THIS BOOK BELONGS TO:

COMPLIMENTS OF:
TELAMON CORPORATION
& R.I.F

First published in Great Britain in 2004 by Andersen Press, Ltd.
First hardcover U.S. edition, 2005
First Hyperion Paperbacks edition, 2007

10   9   8   7   6   5   4   3   2   1

Printed in Singapore

Library of Congress Cataloging-in-Publication Data on file.
ISBN 0-7868-5685-8 (pbk. ed.)

Visit www.hyperionbooksforchildren.com

Shhh!

JEANNE WILLIS and TONY ROSS

HYPERION PAPERBACKS FOR CHILDREN
NEW YORK

A little shrew had wonderful news!
He wanted to tell the whole world,
but it was too noisy:

The shrew had a great big thing to say,
but he only had a very small voice.
No one could hear him above the noise:

rumble,
rumble,
rumble!

The shrew waited all day.
He waited all night for quiet,
but it never came:

Boo

hoo

hoo!

Morning came.

The shrew shouted his news from the roof,
but nobody heard him:

He went to the bottom of the valley,

and tried again,

but still no one heard a word he said:

plop,
plop,
plop!
clip,
clip,
clop.
BUZZ, BUZZ,
BRRING,
BRRING,
brum,
brum,
pop!

The shrew stood on a mountaintop.
He threw back his head and said,

"*Shhhhhhh!*
I know the secret of Peace on Earth!"
But nobody heard the shrew.
The world was too noisy:

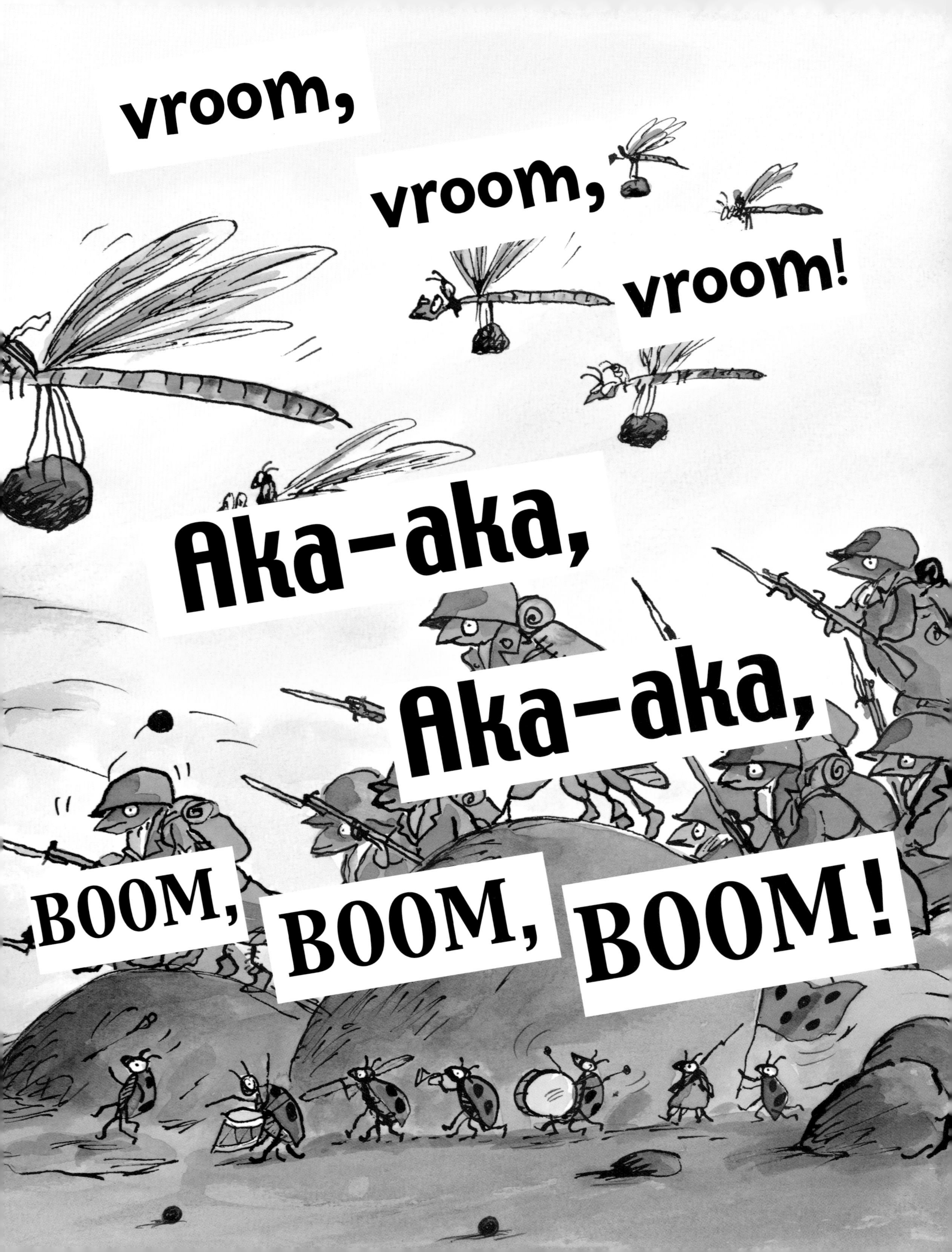

vroom,

vroom,

vroom!

Aka-aka,

Aka-aka,

BOOM, BOOM, BOOM!

But the shrew never gave up.
He hoped that one day,
his voice would be heard.

Maybe if we count to three,
and keep very, very quiet,
perhaps we will hear him.
Shall we try? All together now:

One, two, three . . .

Shhhhhhhhh!

Wonderful news!
You have made a little bit of peace.

Imagine if everyone in the world
sat still and listened just like that:

One, two, three,

Shhhhhhh!

There would be Peace on Earth. . . .

That is the secret.

Or so I've heard.